Lost in the Storm

Clarion Books
a Houghton Mifflin Company imprint
215 Park Avenue South, New York, NY 10003
Copyright © 1974 by Carol and Donald Carrick
All rights reserved.
For information about permission to reproduce
selections from this book, write to Permissions,
Houghton Mifflin Company, 2 Park Street, Boston, MA 02108
Printed in the USA

Library of Congress Cataloging in Publication Data

Carrick, Carol.
    Lost in the storm.

    Summary: Christopher must wait out a long, fretful night
before searching for his dog lost during an island storm.
    [1. Islands—Fiction]   I. Carrick, Donald, Illus.   II. Title.
PZ7.C2344Lo   [E]   74-1051   ISBN 0-395-28776-6

WOZ 10 9 8 7

Lost in the Storm

by CAROL CARRICK

pictures by DONALD CARRICK

CLARION BOOKS
New York

It was a windy day in October. Christopher and his dog, Bodger, waited in the ferryman's shack to keep warm.

The ferryman was watching a Saturday football game, but Christopher was too impatient to watch. He paced back and forth across the little room, with Bodger at his heels.

When Christopher looked out the window, he could see his friend Gray waiting for him on the other side of the channel. Gray lived on the island just off the shore from Christopher's town. No other family lived there during the winter.

"Guess you're the only one who wants to go across this afternoon," said the ferryman. He walked with Christopher up the ramp of the two-car ferry. A few seagulls were standing silently on the dock.

"Today's no day for the beach," the old man said. "Even the birds know enough to stay in town."

"I'm going over to play with Gray this afternoon," Christopher explained. He had just moved from the city, and Gray was the first friend he had made in his new school.

The ferryman steered the tiny ferry into the channel. The water was dark and choppy, with white curls of foam.

"Wind is from the East," shouted the ferryman over the whine of the engine. "It's going to make a really high tide."

As soon as they reached the island, Gray grabbed Christopher
by the arm. "C'mon. Let's play in the boat before it rains."

They righted an overturned rowboat that had been pulled
onshore.

"We can be pirates," said Gray.

Christopher wanted to be the captain, but Gray really knew
how to sail and give sailing orders.

So Christopher suggested, "Let's pretend we've already
landed and we're going to bury our treasure."

Bodger trotted off into the dunes while the boys collected things left by the tide. They discovered a broken picnic basket and filled it with bottles and shells. Their treasure chest grew so heavy they had to drag it.

The clouds were darkening when the boys heard Bodger's hunting bark. Far down the beach they saw his reddish coat in the tall grass. The wind blew sand in their faces and rolled balls of dried seaweed along the beach.

"Look! I can lie down on the wind!" shouted Chris, leaning into it.

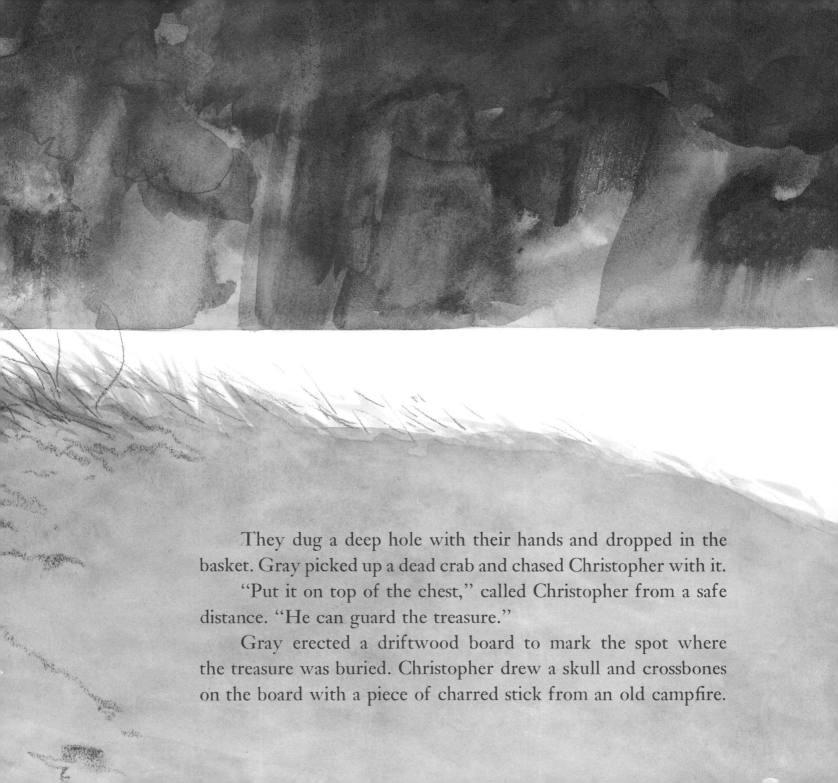

They dug a deep hole with their hands and dropped in the basket. Gray picked up a dead crab and chased Christopher with it.

"Put it on top of the chest," called Christopher from a safe distance. "He can guard the treasure."

Gray erected a driftwood board to mark the spot where the treasure was buried. Christopher drew a skull and crossbones on the board with a piece of charred stick from an old campfire.

Suddenly rain was falling in big drops. The boys ran toward Gray's house, shrieking and laughing.

Gray's father was on the porch looking for them.

"The tide's too high for the ferry to dock," he told Chris. "I called your mother to tell her you would have to stay overnight."

Christopher and Gray danced with delight. They whirled around hugging each other and fell into a heap, giggling.

Then, for the first time, Christopher realized that Bodger hadn't come home with them.

The beach was hidden by the drops that glittered on the porch screen and the sheets of water that spilled from the roof's gutters. Overhead, the pounding rain drowned out the sound of Christopher's voice as he called the dog's name.

Christopher wanted to go looking for Bodger, but Gray's parents wouldn't let him.

"You won't be able to find each other in this storm."

"He'll take care of himself."

"Dogs are smart, you know."

They were both talking at once, trying to convince him.

Gray was silent and his eyes looked troubled. Christopher knew that Gray would have gone out with him if he could. Christopher's own eyes filled with tears. He wasn't ashamed to cry in front of Gray.

Gray's father put an arm around each of them. "Since you guys are already wet, bring in some wood and we'll build a fire."

The boys each carried in an armload of logs from the woodpile. Then Gray's mother hustled them into the bathroom to dry off and change their clothes.

Hamburgers were just going into the frying pan for supper when the lights went out. Everybody gave a shout of surprise.

"The wind must have blown down an electric line," Gray's father said. "Let's do all we can before dark in case the power stays out all night."

They collected candles, a kerosene lantern, and extra blankets. After that was done, Gray's mother kept them busy. They watched the hamburgers grilling in the fireplace and warmed the buns on the hearth. For dessert they toasted marshmallows on long forks.

"The best part is there's no frying pan to wash," said Gray's mother.

The hamburgers were so delicious, and the little house so full of warmth and fun, that Christopher almost forgot about Bodger. But never for very long.

The fire made their faces hot and their eyelids feel heavy. Gray fell asleep on the floor. His mother put him on the couch and covered him without waking him up. She made a cozy bed for Christopher near the fire by pushing two armchairs together.

Christopher lay listening as the wind blew gusts of rain against the windows and whined around the corners of the house. It sounded like the whimper of a dog. He thought about Bodger, wet and hungry.

"He doesn't know how to find me. My trail is lost in the storm."

Several times he crept to the window to look and listen. But there was only the storm outside. Once he fell asleep and dreamed he had found Bodger.

Daylight came as the storm ended. Christopher woke Gray and they quietly left for the beach.

"It will be easier if we walk along the water where the sand is packed down," Gray suggested.

The water had risen high over the beach. The shoreline was so changed that the boys couldn't even find where the treasure was buried.

Then they saw the dog tracks.

"They must be fresh!" yelled Gray. "Last night's tracks would be washed away."

The paw prints ran along the high water mark for a while, then wandered inland where they disappeared. The boys stood on a high dune and looked in all directions. Nothing moved but water and grass.

They continued to walk along the shore. After a while the tracks reappeared, but there was still no dog in sight.

"Look!" shouted Chris. A flight of stairs had been washed up on the beach. Under it they saw Bodger, lying with his head resting on his paws. He lifted it as he heard their voices. The dog galloped toward them, then thundered past. He swerved and returned, jumped on Christopher and knocked him over. When Christopher tried to grab him he pulled away, tearing around Chris in giddy circles, kicking up the sand with his hind legs. And then he was happily all over Christopher, digging his wet nose in his neck.

When they got home, Gray's mother was making waffles. "The power must have come on while we were sleeping," she said.

She stroked Bodger's head. "See, I told you he could take care of himself." But she looked very pleased nevertheless.

She gave the dog a bowl of milk with two raw eggs in it. Bodger drank greedily, splashing the floor.

When it was time to go home, Gray went down to the dock with Christopher. Gulls were gliding in the cloudless sky, and some were picking over stranded shellfish that had washed up onto the dock.

Gray rang the ship's bell to call the ferryman over. Christopher was the only passenger again, but he could see cars lining up on the town side to cross for a day's fishing or beachcombing.

"Hey," the ferryman called, "you're going the wrong way again. Today is beach weather."

"Bodger and I had enough beach," said Christopher sleepily. "We're going home."